I'm going to give you a Bear Hug!

By Caroline B. Cooney

Illustrated by Tim Warnes

ZONDER**kidz**

Bear hugs to Louisa, Sayre, and Harold
–CBC

For my little nephew, Jonah
–TW

ZONDERKIDZ

I'm Going to Give You a Bear Hug
Copyright © 2016 by Caroline B. Cooney
Illustrations © 2016 by Tim Warnes

Requests for information should be addressed to:

Zonderkidz, 3900 Sparks Drive SE, Grand Rapids, Michigan 49546

ISBN 978-0-310-75473-2

Zonderkidz is a trademark of Zondervan.

Design: Kris Nelson

Printed in China

16 17 18 19 20 /LPC/ 20 19 18 17 16 15 14 13 12 11 10 9 8 7 6 5 4 3 2 1

I'm going to give you a bear hug.

A show you how much I care hug.
   A good night,
   Sleep tight,

Way beyond compare hug.

I'm going to give you a dog hug.
A knock over chairs,
Chase up the stairs,

And sleep like a log hug.

I'm going to give you a cat hug.
A simple purr,
Stroke my fur,

Don't do more than that hug.

I'm going to give you a horse hug.

A grab the mane,
Race through rain,
Yes oh yes, of course! hug.

I'm going to give you a duck hug.
A webbed feet,
Feathered seat,

Waddle through the muck hug.

I'm going to give you a pig hug.

A never fail,

Curly tail,

Big, big, big, big, BIG hug.

I'm going to give you a fish hug.
A wet and drippy,
Slimy slippy,

What on earth is <u>this</u>? hug.

I'm going to give you a whale hug.

A high tide,

Ocean wide,

Take me for a sail hug.

I'm going to give you a bug hug.
A wiggly wriggly,
Makes you giggly,

Creepy crawly snug hug.

I'm going to give you a sheep hug.

A lamb's wool,

Blanket full,

Don't make a peep hug.

I'm going to give you a bear hug.

A gasp for air,
All you dare,
Anything that's fair hug.

A just right,
Turn off the light,
Sleep tight,
Say your prayers and kiss good night,

A gasp for air,
All you dare,
Anything that's fair hug.

A just right,
Turn off the light,
Sleep tight,
Say your prayers and kiss good night.

Way beyond compare hug.